PUBLISHED BY DOUBLEDAY
a division of Bantam Doubleday Dell Publishing Group, Inc.
666 Fifth Avenue, New York, New York 10103

DOUBLEDAY and the portrayal of an anchor with a dolphin
are trademarks of Doubleday, a division of
Bantam Doubleday Dell Publishing Group, Inc.

First published in Great Britain in 1989 by
Macmillan Children's Books
a division of Macmillan Publishers Limited
London and Basingstoke
Associated companies throughout the world

Library of Congress Cataloging-in-Publication Data
Inkpen, Mick.
    Gumboot's chocolaty day / Mick Inkpen.
        p.   cm.
    Summary: Gumboot the pig has an exciting outing
    involving hungry ducks
    and his own favorite food, chocolate.
[1. Pigs—Fiction. 2. Ducks—Fiction. 3. Chocolate—Fiction.]
I. Title.
PZ7.I564Gu   1991
[E]—dc20   90-31558   CIP   AC
ISBN 0-385-41489-7
ISBN 0-385-41490-0 (lib. bdg.)
RL: 2.5
Copyright © 1989 by Mick Inkpen
PRINTED IN BELGIUM

MARCH 1991

FIRST EDITION IN THE UNITED STATES OF AMERICA

Gumboot's
chocolaty day

Mick Inkpen

DOUBLEDAY

NEW YORK   LONDON   TORONTO   SYDNEY   AUCKLAND

Gumboot was having a chocolaty sort of day. His aunt had been to visit him and she had given Gumboot a big bar of his favorite chocolate.

"Don't eat it all at once," she had said.

To start with there had been fifteen chunks of chocolate on Gumboot's chocolate bar. Gumboot didn't know this because he could only count to ten.

But what he did know was that he liked chocolate. Very much.

That was why there were now only three pieces left.

Next to chocolate what Gumboot liked best in the world was riding his bike. So he tucked his chocolate safely into the basket and off he went to the park.

In the park Gumboot stopped to watch the ducks on the lake.

Out in the middle, three of them were paddling about with their heads under the water and their tails stuck up in the air. Their curly-tailed bottoms bobbing up and down made Gumboot giggle.

Gumboot wondered how long they could stay down. He began to count from one to ten. When he reached ten the last duck was still down so he began again. Gumboot counted up to ten three times before the last duck popped up out of the water.

"The winner!" shouted Gumboot across the lake.

The duck looked at Gumboot and quacked happily.

"I wonder why ducks never smile," thought Gumboot to himself. Perhaps it was because of their stiff beaks. He tried making his snout stiff to see what it felt like.

Farther along a little girl was throwing bread to the ducks.

"I wonder if ducks like chocolate," thought Gumboot.

Gumboot tried to break off a tiny piece of chocolate to throw to the ducks. But chocolate bars will only break where they want to and in the end Gumboot had to make do with a whole chunk.

"I suppose it's worth it," said Gumboot as he took aim.

But Gumboot's aim was not very good. The piece of chocolate went straight up into the air and landed at the water's edge with a delicious-sounding plop!

The ducks ignored it.

Gumboot was quite pleased. He ran to the spot, fished out the chocolate and popped it safely in his mouth, where it belonged.

"Ducks don't eat chocolate," said a voice. It was the little girl. She was holding out a large piece of bread. "I'll swap you."

Gumboot thought for a moment. There were only two pieces of chocolate left.

"All right then," he said. "You can have one piece and I'll have the other."

The little girl put the chocolate straight in her mouth and gave Gumboot the bread.

Gumboot and the little girl began to feed the ducks.

After a while Gumboot noticed that it was always the same ones who rushed to the bread and grabbed it.

So he tried throwing pieces of bread first one way and then another, which made the ducks paddle backward and forward flapping and quacking.

They made such a noise that soon all the other ducks on the lake were swimming toward them to see what the fuss was about.

Gumboot was having fun. Ducks and bread were flying in all directions.

He tried throwing high throws. Then he tried long throws. And then he broke the bread into lots of little pieces and threw them all at once.

"Get ready everyone!" he shouted. "Here goes the last piece!"

The last piece flew high over the lake and landed in the water with a deep "Gloop!"

"That made a funny noise," thought Gumboot.

Then he realized that something awful had happened. Something terrible. In his excitement he had thrown his chocolate into the lake.

His last piece of chocolate. His only piece of chocolate!

"Never mind," said the little girl.

But Gumboot did mind. He minded very much. He wandered miserably back along the path thinking of his last piece of chocolate lying at the bottom of the lake.

It made him feel hungry.

A tear rolled down his cheek and splashed to the ground.

"Goodbye," called the little girl, but Gumboot didn't seem to hear.

A duck quacked behind him. But Gumboot didn't feel like playing with ducks anymore.

The duck quacked again, this time more loudly. It seemed to be following him.

"Gumboot look!" The little girl was calling and pointing excitedly. "Look in its beak!"

Gumboot turned and looked at the duck. It was the champion diver that he had watched earlier. And in its beak it had something square and brown.

It was Gumboot's last piece of chocolate!

Gumboot took the chocolate and patted the duck on the head. The duck swam round in a little circle quacking loudly and then headed off across the lake.

To Gumboot it seemed that this time the duck was definitely smiling.

"Goodbye!" called Gumboot to the little
girl. She smiled back at him.
Gumboot smiled too. All the way home.

"What a happy thing chocolate is,"
thought Gumboot as he put the last piece
in his mouth. It tasted a little pondy, but
otherwise . . .

. . . delicious!